Juliet
nearly a
Vet

The Lost Dogs

Puffin Books

Juliet
nearly a
Vet

The Lost Dogs

REBECCA JOHNSON

Illustrated by Kyla May

Puffin Books

PUFFIN BOOKS

Published by the Penguin Group
Penguin Group (Australia)
707 Collins Street, Melbourne, Victoria 3008, Australia
(a division of Penguin Australia Pty Ltd)
Penguin Group (USA) Inc.
375 Hudson Street, New York, New York 10014, USA
Penguin Group (Canada)
90 Eglinton Avenue East, Suite 700, Toronto, Canada ON M4P 2Y3
(a division of Penguin Canada Books Inc.)
Penguin Books Ltd
80 Strand, London WC2R 0RL England
Penguin Ireland
25 St Stephen's Green, Dublin 2, Ireland
(a division of Penguin Books Ltd)
Penguin Books India Pvt Ltd
11 Community Centre, Panchsheel Park, New Delhi – 110 017, India
Penguin Group (NZ)
67 Apollo Drive, Rosedale, Auckland 0632, New Zealand
(a division of Penguin New Zealand Pty Ltd)
Penguin Books (South Africa) (Pty) Ltd, Rosebank Office Park, Block D,
181 Jan Smuts Avenue, Parktown North, Johannesburg, 2196, South Africa
Penguin (Beijing) Ltd
7F, Tower B, Jiaming Center, 27 East Third Ring Road North,
Chaoyang District, Beijing 100020, China

Penguin Books Ltd, Registered Offices: 80 Strand, London, WC2R 0RL, England

First published by Penguin Group (Australia), 2014

Cover and text design by Karen Scott © Penguin Group (Australia)
Illustrations by Kyla May Productions
Typeset in New Century Schoolbook
Colour separation by Splitting Image Colour Studio, Clayton, Victoria
Printed and bound in Australia by Griffin Press, an accredited ISO AS/NZS 14001
Environmental Management Systems printer.

National Library of Australia
Cataloguing-in-Publication data:

Johnson, Rebecca.
The Lost Dogs/Rebecca Johnson; illustrated by Kyla May.

ISBN: 978 0 14 330826 3 (pbk.)

A823.4

puffin.com.au

Hi! I'm Juliet. I'm ten years old.
And I'm nearly a vet!

I bet you're wondering how someone who is only ten
could nearly be a vet. It's pretty simple really.
My mum's a vet. I watch what she does and
I help out all the time. There's really not that
much to it, you know...

For my brilliant brother Ray,
for always making me smile. Rx

CHAPTER 1

Dogs know vets will help them

I wake up to a scratching noise, but I try to ignore it. There was a storm last night that kept me awake and I just want to go back to sleep.

'Stop it, Max,' I groan and I bury my head under my pillow. Max is my annoying five-year-old brother and he's crazy about dinosaurs. It's all he thinks about. He's probably playing with his dinosaur toys in the hallway again.

The scratching continues and I'm just about to call out for a second time

when I hear a little whimper. That's
not Max, I think, sitting up in bed.
It's coming from outside.

I go to the front door and look out
through the glass. It's a dog. A really
scruffy, skinny-looking dog. I put my
hand up to the glass and the dog licks
at it from the other side. It must know
I'm nearly a vet.

Vets know they have to be careful
about touching stray dogs, but I can
see this one's friendly and needs help.

I open the front door just a little
and the dog pushes its shaggy, brown
and white face inside. Its tongue is out
of control, trying to find something to
lick. Suddenly Curly, my cocker spaniel,

rushes towards us from the kitchen, barking like crazy.

'Curly! Be quiet!' my Dad's voice booms from my parents' bedroom at the back of the house.

'I've got him, Dad,' I call. 'Go back to sleep.' Dad's not really into pets, so I'm pretty sure *stray* pets aren't going to be his favourite thing either.

I grab Curly by the collar and try to hold him back from the dog, but that just makes him bark even louder and the stray is pushing at the door from the other side. They're too strong for me. They push towards each other until their noses meet. At least then Curly stops barking.

They stand almost frozen with their noses touching. The scruffy dog is much bigger than Curly but it seems more timid and afraid. I open the door a little wider and the big, hairy, brown mess comes in. He and Curly wag their tails and sniff each other all over. They're friends straightaway.

The new dog has no collar. Some people really need a lesson in animal care. I lead Curly into the kitchen and the stray follows along.

I quietly close the kitchen door behind me and assess the situation. I'm going to need my Vet Diary and vet kit to make some observations. I slip off to my room and grab them.

When I come back into the kitchen
the brown dog is wolfing down my dog's
leftover biscuits. Curly's *not* impressed.

I look down at the blank page.

'Well, the first thing you're going to
need is a name,' I say. For some reason,
one pops straight into my head, so
I write it at the top of the page and
begin to make notes.

HECTOR THE DOG

Breed: He is a mixture – a bit like a labrador
crossed with a collie maybe.

Condition: Very skinny with matted hair.
He's smelly and has fleas.

Nature: Hector is a very friendly dog.

I take out my stethoscope and listen to Hector's heartbeat and then I check his eyes and ears. He seems very happy to be touched and examined. Curly keeps pushing his nose into whatever I am doing.

I'll ask Mum to give him a more detailed examination when she wakes up, but the first person I need here is Chelsea, my next-door neighbour and best friend.

Chelsea is nearly a world-famous animal trainer and groomer. She'll be the best person to get Hector ready for his check-up.

I'm worried that if I leave the dogs while I go next door, they'll bark and

wake Mum and Dad. I open the fridge
to look for something they could eat
while I race and get Chelsea.

I push a few things aside until I see
the perfect doggy treat – a large bowl
of leftover casserole. Hector and Curly
look at me and wag their tails happily
as I take it from the fridge.

I hunt around for a second dog bowl,

but I can't find one. I spot Max's dinosaur bowl on the sink.

'That'll do,' I say, as I grab it.

I leave the dogs with their feast while I run to the side of the house and call up to Chelsea's open window. It's hard to call out quietly.

'Chelsea! Chelsea!'

I'm just about to call out again when Chelsea's neat, blonde head appears. She's obviously been asleep but there's still not a hair out of place on her head.

'We've got an emergency! Bring your grooming kit and come to my kitchen. And try to be quiet.'

Chelsea nods and disappears inside. I race back to the kitchen.

CHAPTER
2

Being a vet can be messy

I slowly open the kitchen door and then screw up my nose. The smell of the stray dog is really bad. He's eaten all of his casserole and licked his bowl clean. Curly has tipped the dinosaur bowl over and he's licking his way around peas and chunks of carrot and celery on the floor. Hector watches him closely. He looks more than happy to finish up for Curly when he's done.

I step on a pea with my bare foot and it squashes between my toes. I pull a face and hobble to get a tissue just as Chelsea sneaks in.

She covers her nose and mouth with her hand when she sees and then smells Hector.

'Mind the peas,' I say.

'Whoa!' says Chelsea. 'What a mess!'

'I know,' I say. 'We'll clean it up later. But first, we've got to get this dog clean before Dad sees him. Then Mum can check him over.'

'Where did he come from?'

'I found him at our door this morning.'

'He must have known you were nearly a vet, Juliet.'

We both smile.

'Well, he's too big to lift into the laundry tub where we bath Curly,' says Chelsea.

'How about the bath?' I say.

'Really?' says Chelsea. 'Your mum won't mind having a huge, smelly dog in her bathroom?'

'If we're quick and quiet, she won't even know.'

We grab some plastic jugs and sneak the dogs down the hallway to the bathroom. The smell of Hector in the small room is even worse when we close the door. Chelsea holds a handtowel over her nose, but her eyes are still watering.

I turn on the taps to fill the bath.

'Okay Chelsea, help me lift him in,'
I say, after I've got the water to the
right temperature.

It's a struggle, but eventually we
get the big, filthy mess of a dog in the
bath. I turn off the taps and we begin
to pour jugs of warm water over his
back. Thick rivers of brown water run
off his coat.

Chelsea opens her grooming kit and
gets out a small bottle of dog shampoo.
'We might need to use some of your
shampoo as well,' she says.

I grab a bottle from the shelf and
we start to lather Hector all over. He
loves it and stands very still as we rub
and scrub, massage and comb him.

The muck and filth makes the foam a dark-brown colour.

'Why can't you stand still like this when you have a bath, Curly?' I say, turning to look at my cocker spaniel sulking in the corner. He doesn't look too happy about all the attention Hector is getting.

'What are all those little black dots?' asks Chelsea, peering at some froth on her hands.

'Fleas,' I tell her.

Chelsea leaps to her feet and moves away from the bath.

'Fleas?' she squeaks. 'You didn't tell me he had fleas!' She starts checking her arms and legs.

'Of course Hector's got fleas,
Chelsea – he's a stray dog. You're going
to have to get used to fleas if you want
to be a world-famous groomer and
trainer.'

Suddenly we hear the toilet flush.
We both freeze. There's a tap on the
door.

'Juliet, what are you doing?'

It's Mum.

'Um, we have an emergency, Mum,' I stammer. 'A stray dog came to our house and . . .'

Just as Mum opens the bathroom door, Hector decides to shake. The whole room is suddenly sprayed with

chocolate-coloured, flying, foamy flea-bombs. We all scream. Mum comes in and quickly shuts the door behind her.

'Juliet, what *were* you thinking? Where did it come from? Is that my *good* shampoo?'

'Mum, calm down!' My voice is almost as hysterical as hers. 'We'll clean it all up. He came to our door. We didn't use that much.'

'Is everything all right, Rachel?' Dad is on the other side of the door.

'Yep,' says Mum, glaring at me. 'It will be. Just give us a minute, love.'

'Why would you bath it in here?' Mum whispers through gritted teeth. 'Why didn't you come and get me?

Why didn't you wash it outside?'

I can't keep up with Mum's questions. She's so cross I don't actually think she wants an answer. She takes the jug from me and starts to rinse Hector.

'You girls start wiping down the walls and floor. And put Curly outside.'

When I open the bathroom door to take Curly out, I hear more trouble coming from the kitchen.

'Aw, yuck! What's this all over the floor?' Dad has found the peas, carrot and celery.

'Gross. What's all this brown stuff?' Max has found his dinosaur bowl.

Being a vet can be very complicated.

CHAPTER 3

Being a vet can be tough

'There is no way that dog is staying here!' Dad is not happy about our unexpected visitor.

'I agree,' says Mum. 'I don't think I've seen him at the surgery before, but I'll check and see if we can find his home.' She turns to look at Chelsea and me. 'If we can't, Hector will have to go to the lost dogs' home. If someone's looking for him, that'll be the first place they go.'

Chelsea is still trying to comb the

knots out of Hector's fur. 'If someone did own him, they didn't look after him very well,' she says.

We go with Mum to her surgery and she checks Hector over. He's thin, but other than that, he's healthy enough. Mum lets me scan him for a microchip but he doesn't have one.

'What are microchips anyway?' asks Chelsea.

'They're made from silicon and are about the size of a grain of rice,' I tell her. 'Microchips are injected into an animal's loose skin and each chip has a special code to show who owns it. The codes are read with a scanner like this one.' I pass the scanner to Chelsea, so she can have a turn. 'They're really good if a dog loses its collar.'

Mum double-checks her files, but a dog matching Hector's description has never come into her surgery.

Chelsea and I spend a few hours making Hector look and feel better. We brush him and trim the fur around his eyes and mouth. We even clean his teeth!

Curly has a bath too, in case he picked up some of Hector's fleas. We do it in a large plastic tub that Dad has put outside for us. He's not in the mood for dogs inside after this morning.

Curly stands very still for his bath, which is unusual. He keeps looking over at Hector as Chelsea brushes his coat and quietly talks to him. I think Curly might be just a bit jealous, so I give him a big hug to make him feel special, too.

When both dogs are pampered and beautiful, we tie a lovely blue bow around Hector's neck and take them

for a walk down the street. We stop to talk with every person we meet, but nobody has seen Hector before.

We're both exhausted and very disappointed when we get home.

'Poor Hector,' says Chelsea. 'I don't want to take him to the lost dogs' home. But what can we do?'

'Maybe we could take his photo and make some lost dog posters to put up around the neighbourhood?' I suggest.

We get busy and make a heap of posters. Dad even lets us print them out on his good printer. I think he wants Hector to find his home as much as we do.

We all admire our work as the

HAVE YOU LOST THIS FRIENDLY DOG?

HE WAS FOUND IN DAISY RD ON SATURDAY MORNING. HE IS WELL BEHAVED AND HAPPY TO EAT HIS VEGETABLES WITH HIS DINNER.

PLEASE CALL 98 873 0384 IF YOU KNOW WHERE HE COMES FROM.

printer spits out the copies.

Dad drives us around to put the posters up on posts and walls.

'He can sleep in the garage tonight, but tomorrow we'll have to take him to the lost dogs' home,' says Mum when we get back. 'Sorry, girls, but no one has rung about him.'

I look down and sadly pat Hector's

head as he wags his tail.

'We can't keep him, Juliet. I know it's really hard and very sad, but we can't keep every lost animal that comes in. The lost dogs' home will find him somewhere nice to live.'

I understand that we can't keep him, but when I look at Hector I just want to cry.

He's lying on the floor with his head on Max's lap. Max is showing him his dinosaur collection. I can see Hector loves us already. Why else would he put up with looking at all of Max's dinosaurs?

'We could ask your mum?' I say to Chelsea hopefully.

'I already tried. Twice,' says Chelsea.
'Mum says it wouldn't be fair on
Princess and she's probably right.'

I understand why Chelsea's mum
said no. Princess is Chelsea's kitten.
Her mother was a stray cat we saved
once. Princess *really* doesn't like dogs.

Mum lets us give Hector an extra
big dinner and we set up a bed for
him in the garage. Chelsea's sleeping
over tonight and we sit together with
him until it's time for bed. He cries a
bit when we shut the door but after a
while he settles down.

Later that night I'm woken up by
another thunderstorm. I can hear

Hector, above all the wind and rain, crying in the garage. I don't know how Chelsea can sleep through all the noise. I put on my dressing gown and Curly and I go and sit with him until the storm passes.

Being a vet can be really sad at times. Someone out there must want a beautiful dog like Hector.

CHAPTER 4

Vets know how to be helpful

The next morning we put Hector in the car and drive to the Mercy Street Home for Lost Dogs. When we get out of the car, the barking from inside the building is crazy. Hector doesn't want to go in and I don't blame him.

Chelsea and I need Mum's help to get him to walk to the entrance and he strains against his leash.

'He hates it here already, Mum.' I can feel myself getting upset again.

'Let's just go in and see what they

think,' says Mum gently.

There's no one at the front counter but there's a bell. Mum rings it and we stand and wait. Chelsea sits with Hector, her arms around his neck.

After quite a long time, a man slides the side door open and enters the room. The sound of the dogs barking is even louder until he shuts it again.

'Sorry to keep you waiting,' he says. 'It's been very busy this weekend. Always is after a storm.'

'We're sorry to add to your load,' says Mum, 'but this dog showed up at our house. I don't suppose anyone has reported a large, shaggy, brown dog missing?'

The man looks at Hector and runs his finger down his list as he wipes his forehead with the back of his arm. I look more closely at him. He has a very kind face but he looks really tired.

'Nope,' he says. 'No brown shaggy dogs on the list. Doesn't mean they won't call though. It was such a whopper of a storm last night *and* the night before that I've got dogs here from two towns away! Of course, it had to happen when I'm short on staff. Two of them are on holidays until next week.'

'I'm a vet,' says Mum. 'Can I give you a hand?'

'Are you kidding?' says the man.

'I would love an extra hand. Just having someone help to check over them all and see if they have microchips or any injuries would be so helpful.'

'I'm nearly a vet and Chelsea is nearly a world-famous animal trainer and groomer,' I say. 'Can we help, too?'

The man looks at Mum. She smiles and nods her head. 'They're actually a great help to me around the surgery.'

'Well, that's settled then,' says the man, smiling. 'What good luck to have three experts to help me out!'

Mum calls Dad to tell him we're going to help out for the day. She says Dad was very pleased because

he thought she was ringing to say
Hector was coming back home.

Chelsea and I race out to the car
to get our vet and grooming kits.
We never leave home without them.
Vets and groomers always need to be
prepared for emergencies.

The man tells us his name is Paul
and then he leads us into the area
where the dogs are kept.

There are dogs in cages everywhere.
Big dogs, little dogs, long dogs, short
dogs, white dogs, black dogs, spotty
dogs and patchy dogs. I had no idea so
many dogs could get lost.

'It's not normally this bad,' says
Paul, yelling over the barking. 'And

twelve people have already rung to say they're coming for their dogs. Can you believe that before the storm, I only had four dogs here?' Paul opens the last cage on the left where there is a chubby cream-coloured labrador.

We lead Hector inside and they both wag their tails and sniff each other's noses. Maybe he won't mind being here after all? I think. But then Hector turns around and looks back at us through the wire of the cage. He starts to cry.

'It's okay, Hector,' I say, patting him through the wire. He must feel really confused.

Paul sees that I am starting to get upset. 'Hector will be fine,' he says.

'He'll settle down soon.'

'Let's help Paul get these other dogs sorted out and then we can work out where Hector belongs,' says Mum, giving me a hug.

Being a vet can be very emotional.

Paul nods. 'I need to check them all for microchips so we can let the other dog pounds and refuges know what dogs we have here. Then we'll put the dogs that have been claimed into the cages up near the office and bath the ones that are really dirty. Plus they're all going to need food, water, fresh bedding and a walk.'

I whip out my Vet Diary and make some notes.

- Sort out which dogs have been claimed and which ones are still lost.
- Give dirty dogs a bath.
- Feed them.
- Fill up water bowls.
- Get clean bedding for each dog.
- Take dogs for a walk.

'Okay,' says Mum, looking around at the dozens of barking, howling, wagging dogs. 'Let's get to work. Where shall we start?'

Paul races to the office and comes back with his list. 'Girls, if I put a peg on the gate of a cage, it means that dog's owner has been found and they are friendly enough for you to handle.

Here are some leashes. If you could walk them to the empty cages up near the office and check they have food, water and bedding, they'll be fine to wait there for their owners to collect them.'

'Rachel, if you would give me a hand to check all of the unclaimed dogs for injuries and microchips, that would be great.'

'If only Hector had a microchip,' sighs Chelsea.

'Or a collar,' I say.

We both look through the cage at Hector. He stands and wags his tail at us hopefully. I wonder if anyone has ever loved him at all.

CHAPTER
5

Being a vet can be a dirty job

Chelsea and I start moving the dogs with pegs on their cages. We can't help giving them a quick cuddle as we move each of them into their new pens.

'You're going home,' says Chelsea, hugging a fluffy little white dog that wriggles in her arms. 'Yes, you are! Yes, you are!'

A big black labrador with a fancy blue collar with a silver tag that says 'Gus' is next. It takes both of us ages to get Gus to go into his pen and then he's halfway out again before we can shut the gate. I'm about to call out to Paul to help us but then I see he and Mum are busy with a big spotty Dalmatian in the far pen.

'I've got an idea,' says Chelsea, and she runs to the feed area and grabs a bowl of pellets. 'Maybe this will tempt him.'

'No wonder you're nearly a world-famous animal trainer and groomer,' I laugh, as Gus obediently follows Chelsea into his pen and starts to wolf down his food.

A sausage dog is next, then a poodle, then a dog that looks like a mix of ten breeds.

At last all of the claimed dogs have been moved. We bring bowls of food and water and a soft blanket for each one. Some of the little dogs don't want to eat but Paul says not to worry because their owners will be here soon.

Next Chelsea and I turn our attention to the six dogs that need bathing. Paul has a very large bathing area that has a showerhead on a hose and a big tub.

'This beats our bathroom,' I whisper to Chelsea and we both laugh.

Chelsea and I decide that I'll bring her the dogs after I've given them a quick check-up and then she'll bath them. After their bath I'll dry them off and give them food and water and clean bedding.

Our first dog is an Australian terrier. He's a solid little thing with stringy brown and black fur that's covered in mud and burrs. Apart from this he seems fine, so I bring him in for a bath. Chelsea is wearing white and I grimace as I hand her the muddy, wet dog.

In no time at all Chelsea has him looking super clean and passes him back to me wrapped in a towel. She really does have a talent for washing dogs. I pass her the next dog and take the terrier back for drying and feeding. Our system works very well and in no time at all we have four very clean dogs.

Next up is a dog that looks like a border collie crossed with something else. It's sitting very quietly in the corner. When I clip on the lead he pulls against it.

'It's all right,' I say, patting him gently. 'We won't hurt you.'

I notice he's shaking and holding up his paw. When I take a closer look I can

see he's caught his dew claw on something and it's bleeding and hanging off.

I grab my Vet Diary and turn back to the page on dew claws to remind myself of what needs to be done. (Mum told me about them once.)

DEW CLAWS:

- Dew claws on a dog are kind of like a thumb, or a big toe on a human.
- They are about 5cm up on the side of a dog's paw.
- Sometimes they're removed because they can catch on things and this can be very painful for the poor dog.

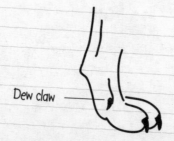

Dew claw

When I find Mum she is running
the microchip scanner over a big dog
while Paul holds the dog steady.

'Mum, one of the dogs has ripped its
dew claw and it's bleeding pretty badly.
I think it might need surgery.'

'Oh, okay,' says Mum. 'I'll come right
away.'

Paul looks at me and nods. I can
see he is impressed that I know what
a dew claw is, but then again every
vet would.

'You're right, Juliet. This little guy
needs surgery to fix that claw,' says
Mum, gently stroking the dog. 'He'll
have to come back with me so it's done

properly. We'll need to bandage his paw up for now. My emergency kit's in the boot of the car, but I know I'm short of bandages. I meant to get some more yesterday.'

'Don't worry, Mum,' I say. 'I've got heaps.' I snap open my vet kit and hold up three bandages of different sizes.

'I'm so lucky you're nearly a vet,' says Mum, smiling. 'But that also explains where all my bandages have gone!'

We watch while Mum bandages the dog's paw and then she takes it to a pen to have a rest until it's time to go.

I look over at Chelsea who has

found an apron from somewhere and still looks incredibly clean and tidy. I haven't washed a dog all day and my clothes are covered in dog hair and spots of mud. How does she do it?

'This is the last one,' I say, passing her a little black ball of fluff with sad eyes. He is shaking all over and obviously doesn't like baths.

'Come on now,' says Chelsea. 'It's nice and warm and we won't hurt you.'

'I might have to hold him,' I say, as the dog leaps around in the tub. When he's wet he looks like a drowned rat and he's really hard to hold still. At one stage he tries to leap out of the bath and knocks the hose out of

Chelsea's hands. Water sprays straight into my face.

'Oops!' says Chelsea. 'Sorry!'

Both the dog and I are sopping wet, but we're also a lot cleaner.

I look back down at our list to see what's next. There are a lot of jobs I can tick off.

LOST DOG JOBS:

- Sort out which dogs have been claimed and which ones are still lost. ✓
- Give dirty dogs a bath. ✓
- Feed them. ✓
- Fill up water bowls. ✓
- Get clean bedding for each dog.
- Take dogs for a walk.

CHAPTER
6

Vets have lots of good ideas

'Time to take them for a walk,' says
Chelsea.

'It'll be good for them to dry off,'
I say. 'And me!'

We go and see how Mum and Paul
are going.

Everything looks more orderly now.

'Thank goodness for microchips,'
says Paul. 'Nineteen out of the twenty-
eight dogs have homes we can find.
I have all the microchip numbers so
I'll get their details online and start

contacting the owners.'

The dogs have stopped barking and Paul looks much more relaxed than he did this morning. 'You guys have done an amazing job. I could never have done it on my own. Thank you so much,' he says.

'I'll pop back to my surgery with the dog that needs the dew claw removed. It can stay there overnight,' says Mum.

'Is it okay if we take the lost dogs for a short walk to dry them off?' I ask. 'You never know, someone might recognise one of them.'

'It's fine by me,' says Paul. 'That would be a great help.'

'How about you just walk them to

the end of this street and back?' says
Mum. 'And don't take too many at
once. I'll come back for you in about
two hours.'

Chelsea and I choose two dogs each for
the first trip. I choose the fat labrador
and Hector, and Chelsea chooses the
little terrier and the black fluffy dog.

Before we leave, Chelsea puts a
few finishing touches on them. Each
dog is brushed and styled and given
a different-coloured bow to wear
around its neck. No wonder Chelsea's
nearly world-famous, those dogs look
fantastic.

We head off down the street with

our flash-looking pooches. It's quite tricky keeping them all together because they all want to sniff and wee on everything. Luckily we don't have to walk far until we come to a bowls club.

There are heaps of people there. They can't help but stop to admire the dogs. Hector's very happy to meet them all. He wags his tail and circles around them. He gets the most pats because he just loves people. The labrador just wants to sniff their pockets for food.

'Oh, I do miss having a little dog,' says one old lady, bending down to scoop up Chelsea's little black ball of fur. 'We're not allowed to have dogs in the retirement home where I live.'

'They're all lost. We have to try to find their homes,' says Chelsea.

'And if they don't have homes, we need to find them new ones,' I add.

'They seem like nice dogs. It's a pity they're lost,' says an old man. 'Do you

girls work at the lost dogs' home?'

'No, we're just helping out today.
We're on school holidays, but we have
to go back to school in a week.' I let
out a sigh.

We eventually get the dogs past the
bowls club and walk them up to the
corner and back. There are more people

waiting to say hello to us on the return trip. The dogs love the attention and it seems the older people love giving it. They're all laughing and patting the dogs and telling stories about the pets they once owned.

They're even more excited when we say we'll be bringing another lot.

When we get back to Paul there are three cars parked outside the lost dogs' home and lots of happy people at the front desk. They must have been very worried. I can't imagine what it would be like to lose Curly.

We don't want to disturb Paul when he's so busy, so we swap the dogs over and start to groom the next four.

This time I have the large spotty Dalmatian and a smaller shaggy dog and Chelsea has a sausage dog and a poodle. We head out through the front office again. The lost dogs look very smart with their bows.

'I've never seen dogs from a pound look so lovely,' says one lady to her friend as they watch us walk by.

'I must tell my sister to come and look here. She's looking for a new dog after her poor old Snooky died.'

'Chelsea,' I say, 'that lady has just given me an idea.'

'What?'

'Well, lots of people forget that you can get lovely dogs from pet shelters.

Dogs that are just as nice as dogs from other places, and a lot cheaper, too.'

'You're right,' says Chelsea.

'Well, maybe we need to make more posters like the one we made for Hector? We could put them in pet supply shops and in Mum's surgery. They might even put them in the paper!'

'Juliet, that's brilliant. No wonder you're nearly a vet.'

'Let's start making posters when we get home tonight. Mum has a camera on her phone so we can take some snaps of them before we leave.'

We're so excited talking about our new idea that we're back at the bowls club before we know it. The manager of the bowls club has carried some chairs out to the footpath and there is now a row of smiling faces and warm hands waiting to say hello to us.

We tell them about our idea for the posters and a lady with a long grey plait suggests putting posters in the bowls club too.

When we finally get back to Paul we're exhausted, and Mum drives in just us we unclip the last of the dogs.

'Great news,' says Paul. 'The Australian terrier has been picked up as well, so that leaves us with just eight homeless pooches. Hopefully more of those will go in the next couple of days.'

I smile, even though I was hoping it was Hector that had found his home.

Maybe more posters will help him.

'Paul, can we make some posters about the dogs that need to find a home? We thought it might help.'

'That's a great idea,' says Paul. 'I can copy them and put them on our website, too.'

'Can we come back tomorrow?' I beg Mum. 'Chelsea and I are really going to need to get to know the dogs if we're going to make meaningful posters about them.'

'And they will definitely need more walking and grooming,' adds Chelsea.

'Sure,' say Mum, rolling her eyes just a little. 'As long as it's okay with you, Paul? I have to bring the other dog back anyway.'

'Of course it is!' says Paul. 'How often do I have assistants who are nearly vets and groomers to help me out?'

Chelsea and I can't get the smiles off our faces. We're going to be very busy.

CHAPTER 7

Vets stay up late sometimes

Before we leave the Mercy Street Home for Lost Dogs we get Mum to take some photos of the dogs that need to find a family.

As soon as we get home, we race to Mum's surgery to check on the dog with the sore paw. He's still a bit sleepy from his operation, but Mum says he's going to be fine.

Curly is not too happy when he sniffs our clothes. He can smell other dogs all over us and seems a bit confused.

After we've had a shower and dinner, we load the photos onto the computer and start to make our posters.

'If we put the dog's photo at the top, we can make a checklist to fill out when we observe them tomorrow,' I suggest.

'Great idea,' agrees Chelsea. 'That way people get a quick snapshot of what each dog is like.'

We start to make our checklist.

Name:
Age: Puppy / adult / mature
Sex: Male / Female
Eating habits: eats anything / fussy eater
Likes:
☐ Exercise   ☐ Chewing things
☐ Baths   ☐ Barking
☐ Chasing balls   ☐ Older people
☐ Sleeping   ☐ Vegetables
☐ Children

'Time for bed, girls,' says Mum.

Chelsea is sleeping over at my house – I love school holidays.

'Nearly finished, Mum,' I say. 'Can we just have a couple more minutes?'

'Five minutes, then into bed.'

Curly is snuggled up on the floor beside us. I give him a big cuddle.

He's very happy being the top dog again. I hope Hector's not too sad.

'At the bottom we should say to contact the Mercy Street Home for Lost Dogs and include the phone number,' I say.

'Good idea,' says Chelsea, and she types it in.

We fall into bed exhausted. For once, we are both too tired to talk.

Curly wakes me the next morning by licking my toes.

'Yuck, Curly!' I laugh.

We have breakfast and then go out to Mum's surgery to check on the collie with the sore paw.

Mum lets us take him out for a bit of a walk in the garden before we put him in the car to go back to the lost dogs' home.

'I wonder if anyone else has rung about their dog?' says Chelsea on our way there.

I know Chelsea is thinking about Hector as much as I am. Best friends know these things.

When we get there we can tell lots of dogs have gone home because it's heaps quieter.

'We're down to just six now,' Paul reports happily. 'One of the other shelters called looking for the little poodle and the small shaggy dog.'

'Can we go and see Hector?'

'Sure,' says Paul, and he stays to talk to Mum about the collie with the sore foot.

Hector is curled up on a blanket when we go in. A lot of the other dogs jump up and run to the front of their pens, but he doesn't move.

'Hector,' I whisper quietly as we open his door.

Hector leaps up when he hears my voice. He jumps all over both of us and turns around in happy circles. Chelsea and I hug him as hard as we can.

'Come on, Hector,' says Chelsea. 'Let's see what you lost dogs can do.'

CHAPTER
8

Animal trainers are really clever

Paul helps us take the six dogs out
into the large yard behind the shed to
start our observations.

We tie the dogs to the fence in a line
and I sit with a clipboard while Chelsea
ties a number on a piece of card around
each dog's neck. Paul obviously hasn't
seen a trainer as good as Chelsea
before, so he sits down to watch.

'Let's start with the food tests,'
says Chelsea.

She opens her training kit and

takes out some parcels of different food she has brought from home.

'Um, Chelsea, will your mum mind that you've brought roast lamb, sausages *and* half her vegetables?'

'That's one of the best things about having four huge, football-playing brothers, Juliet. If food disappears, I'm the last person anyone would suspect.'

I nod and look over at Paul. He shrugs his shoulders and frowns a little, but I'm sure he understands that animal trainers must put their animals first.

'Paul, do you have any dry and canned dog food we could use, please?' asks Chelsea.

'Sure. We've got heaps in the shed.'
Paul walks off and soon comes back
with some dog food.

'Okay, let's start with the dry food,'
says Chelsea as she puts a few biscuits
in each dog's bowl. 'When I put them
down, Juliet, could you make a note of
what dog eats what food?'

'Okay,' I say, pencil ready.

She puts the bowls on the ground in
front of each dog. I watch carefully as
the dogs approach their bowls. Some
of them are straight into the dry food,
while others sniff and look away.

Chelsea holds up the next sample
of food and does the same. She keeps
going until the dogs have tried all of

the different foods.

Hector and the labrador love being tested. They're tied up on either side of the little sausage dog. As soon as they finish their food, they strain on their leads to reach his. The sausage dog looks very worried – maybe he thinks he'll be mistaken for a meal!

I draw up a table in my Vet Diary.

Dog number	Breed	Dry food	Canned food	Vegies	Cooked sausage	Roast lamb
1	Dalmation	√	√		√	√
2	Black fluffy dog					√
3	Hector (Mixed breed)	√	√	√	√	√
4	Sausage dog				√	√
5	Labrador	√	√	√	√	
6	Border collie		√		√	

'From this test we can see who's fussy and who isn't,' says Chelsea. 'It'll be really helpful when people enquire about the dogs, Paul. It would be terrible for someone to choose a dog they don't fully understand.'

Paul nods. He has a slightly dazed expression on his face. He's obviously

never seen a world-famous animal
trainer in action before.

'Now let's test some of their other
skills and interests,' says Chelsea.

The phone rings and Paul has to
leave as Chelsea takes some balls and
toys from her bag. She unclips all of the
dogs and throws the tennis ball

down to the other end of the enclosure.

The collie and the Dalmatian take off after it. The sausage dog runs the other way. The black fluffy dog just stares at the other dogs, and the fat labrador sits down and yawns. Hector spends his whole time trying to get as many pats from us as he can.

I take lots of notes as Chelsea continues. She hands the dogs a variety of chew toys that can have food hidden inside them. Only the Dalmatian and Hector show any interest, but Hector has no idea how to get the food from inside the toy. He drops it on the ground in front of him and starts to whimper. The collie is still jumping around waiting for the ball to be thrown again. And the labrador is stretched out and sleeping in the sun.

'Well, this tells me quite a lot,' says Chelsea as she looks down at my notes. 'We can fill in their posters with a lot more detail now. I think the little dogs might suit older people and perhaps the labrador, too. I also think poor Hector has never been given much attention.'

OBSERVATIONS

- The border collie and the Dalmatian can fetch.
- The labrador likes to sleep.
- The Dalmatian and Hector like to chew things.
- The smaller dogs are not very interested in toys or games.
- Hector loves people!

Chelsea is interrupted when Paul calls out to us from the office, 'Girls, the owner of the sausage dog and the black fluffy dog just called. It's an old lady whose friend saw you walking them past the bowls club.'

'Chelsea, you're amazing. You said those little dogs might belong to an older person!' I say, scooping up the sausage dog and giving it a hug. 'Fancy them coming from the same home.'

We update the remaining dogs' posters and then make some copies.

'Let's take them for another walk and put some posters up,' I say. 'Somebody's got to want these lovely dogs!'

CHAPTER 9

Every dog deserves a good home

'You know, Chelsea,' I say quietly, as we walk down the road, 'the dog I'm most worried about is Hector.' I have to whisper because I don't want him to hear me. 'He doesn't really have any talents, except that he loves people.'

'I know,' says Chelsea sadly. 'I really wish we could keep him.'

We get to the bowls club and see a few familiar faces. There doesn't seem to be as many people here today, but a couple of people come out to say hello and pat the dogs.

'Oh, I'm so pleased,' says a little old lady when we tell her some of the dogs have found their homes. 'Every dog deserves a good home.'

Suddenly Hector pricks up his ears and starts to bark.

'Hector, stop it,' I say. He's being a bit naughty now and pulling on his lead. 'Sit!' He just looks at me and coughs from all his pulling. Poor Hector hasn't even been taught how to sit.

The manager comes over to say hello and he offers to put some posters inside the bowls club. He's about to tell us something else when Hector starts pulling and barking again.

'Hector, stop it,' I say. Chelsea leans over to help me hold the lead. He's really going crazy now, jumping around and barking and carrying on.

'Hector, stop it!' I say firmly. I'm embarrassed because he's not making a good impression at all. People expect vets to be good at controlling animals.

Hector won't listen. He is pulling so hard we're being dragged down the path. The other dogs are pulling against us in the opposite direction. Hector is scaring them and creating a huge fuss. People have stopped bowling and are looking over at us.

'Hector! Cut it out!' I yell. Hector spins around so his head is pointing towards us and he's pulling backwards.

'His collar!' Chelsea gasps, just as he pulls it straight over his head and tears off down the street.

'HECCTTTOOOORRRR!' we bellow in unison as the barking dog runs through the carpark and disappears around the back of the bowls club. We can still hear him barking like crazy.

'Please, hold these!' I beg as we pass the leashes of the other three dogs to the people standing with us. I start to panic. I can't bear the thought of Hector getting lost all over again. Being a vet can be terrifying.

We run in the direction of the

barking. The manager follows us.
Maybe he's worried Hector's going to
attack someone.

'I think he's stopped running,'
Chelsea says as we race through the
parked cars.

We turn the corner to see Hector
standing next to something, barking
and wagging his tail. It's an old man.
He's fallen over on the stairs.

'Hector,' says Chelsea. 'Is this what
you were trying to tell us?'

The manager quickly helps the man
up into a sitting position. 'Are you
okay, Bernie?' he asks.

'I'm all right,' says Bernie. 'I'm just
a silly old fool for misjudging those

stairs. I've twisted my ankle.' He leans over and gives Hector a big pat then says, 'I thought I'd be lying here for ages until someone heard me, but this fellow found me straightaway!'

Hector wags his tail happily.

'Well, I'll be darned,' says the manager. 'What a clever dog! You know,

girls, when we were on the footpath
I was just about to tell you the bowls
club has decided to adopt a dog. Lots of
these people live in retirement homes
where they're not allowed to keep pets,
so we thought it'd be nice if there was
a dog here. I was going to choose the
Dalmatian, but I've just changed my
mind. I live at the house attached to
the side there, so at night he could
stay with me.'

'Oh, Hector! Did you hear that?'
Chelsea and I are hugging him all
over. 'Did you hear, Hector? You have a
home. You'll never run out of pats here.
And you'll be close by so we can visit!'

Some more people come and help

Bernie to his feet and we all walk back around to the front of the club.

The manager tells us he'll come to sign Hector's papers and pick him up this afternoon.

We can't wait to tell Paul the good news and we run with the dogs all the way back to the lost dogs' home.

As we walk in I hear Paul telling a family that the dogs at this shelter have all been assessed for their behaviour and food choices. He's showing them our posters about each dog.

I have a feeling it won't be long before the other dogs find homes too!

Right now, it feels *so* good to be nearly a vet.

Quiz! Are You Nearly a Vet?

1. **Dogs often run away in storms because:**
   a. They love the feeling of rain on their fur
   b. They are frightened of thunder
   c. They want a better view of the lightning
   d. They want to meet up with other runaway dogs

2. **Dogs get fleas:**
   a. To give themselves something to scratch
   b. Because they love baths
   c. Because the fleas want to suck blood from the dog
   d. So they don't feel lonely

3. **What should you do if you find a lost dog?**
   a. Check it for a collar
   b. Call the pound to see if someone is missing it
   c. Visit a vet to see if it has a microchip
   d. All of the above

4. **Microchips are:**
   a. Inserted in the dog's ear
   b. Attached to the dog's collar
   c. Swallowed by the dog
   d. Injected under the dog's skin on its neck

5. **Dog shelters:**
   a. Try to find homes for lost dogs
   b. Are often very noisy places
   c. Care a lot about dogs
   d. All of the above

6. **A Dalmatian has:**
a. Long curly brown hair
b. Short white hair with black spots
c. Very long, red whiskers
d. Tiny feet and black straight hair

7. **Which of these is not a small breed of dog?**
a. Labrador
b. Australian terrier
c. Miniature poodle
d. Sausage dog

8. **Dew claws are sometimes removed because:**
a. They catch on things
b. They don't look good with nail polish
c. Other dogs make fun of them
d. Vets like doing operations for fun

9. **How did Juliet meet Hector?**
a. Her dad brought him home from work
b. He came to her front door
c. He snuck into Max's bed
d. He booked himself in to the vet surgery

10. **Every day, dogs need:**
a. Food
b. Water
c. Somewhere warm to sleep
d. All of the above

Answers : 1b, 2c, 3d, 4d, 5d, 6b, 7a, 8a, 9b, 10d. Well done!

. . . . Collect all the **Juliet** *nearly a* **Vet** books!

The Great Pet Plan

My best friend Chelsea and I ♥ animals.
I have a dog Curly and two guinea pigs, but
we need more pets if I'm going to learn to be
a vet. Today, we had the best idea ever. . .
We're going to have a pet sleepover!

At the Show

Chelsea and I are helping our friend, Maisy,
get her pony ready for the local show. But
Midgie is more interested in eating than in
learning to jump (sigh). Pony training is a bit
more difficult than we thought!

Farm Friends

It's Spring and all the animals on Maisy's farm
are having babies. Maisy says I can stay for a
whole week and help out. There are chicks and
ducklings hatching, orphan lambs to feed, and
I can't wait for Bella to have her calf!

Bush Baby Rescue

A terrible bushfire has struck and Mum's vet
clinic is in chaos. Every day more and more
injured baby animals arrive. Chelsea and I
have never been busier! But who knew that
babies needed so much feeding. I may never
sleep again!

Beach Buddies

It's the holidays and we're going camping by the beach. I can't wait to toast marshmallows by the campfire, swim in the sea and explore the rock pools – there are so many amazing animals at the beach.

Zookeeper for a Day

I've won a competition to be a zookeeper for a day! My best friend Chelsea is coming too. I can't wait to learn all about the zoo animals. There will be meerkats, tigers and penguins to feed. And maybe some zoo vets who need some help (I won't forget my vet kit!).

The Lost Dogs

There was a huge storm last night and now there are lots of lost dogs. One turned up outside my window (he must have known I'm nearly a vet). Luckily, Chelsea, Mum and I are helping out at the lost dogs' home.

Playground Pets

Chelsea and I have such a cool school – we get to have playground pets! Guinea pigs, lizards, fish and insects are all part of our science room. But this week, we have a replacement teacher, and Miss Fine doesn't know much about animals. Luckily we do (it's so handy being nearly a vet).

From Rebecca Johnson

During my lifetime I have been very lucky to have had lots of different dogs as much-loved pets. All of them have lived long and happy lives and filled our home with love and laughter. One little dog, Scruffy, chose us when he turned up wet, flea-bitten and scrawny in the middle of a storm. We tried and tried to find his owner, but never did, so we kept him as our own. He was the most faithful, lovely little dog and lived with us for more than ten happy years.

From Kyla May

As a little girl, I always wanted to be a vet. I had mice, guinea pigs, dogs, goldfish, sea snails, sea monkeys and tadpoles as pets. I loved looking after my friends' pets when they went on holidays, and every Saturday I helped out at a pet store.

Now that I'm all grown up, I have the best job in the world. I get to draw lots of animals for children's books and for animated TV shows. In my studio I have two dogs, Jed and Evie, and two cats, Bosco and Kobe, who love to watch me draw.